THE MIDDLE IS THE BEST PART!

Lynette Samuel, Author

Leigh Capps, Illustrator

Patty Baker, Creative Consultant

Bright Lamb Publishers®

BOOKS TO STRENGTHEN RELATIONSHIPS

First Edition

Library of Congress Cataloging-in-Publication Data:
Library of Congress Catalog Card Number: 96-086479
Samuel, Lynette
        The Middle is the Best Part/ by Lynette Samuel; illustrated by Leigh Capps

Summary: Lydia finds herself in the middle of trouble over and over again which convinces her how terrible it is to be the
middle child. When Dad comes home, he reveals that great things are found in the middle.

ISBN 0-9651270-2-8 (book) — ISBN 0-9651270-3-6 (gift package)
[1. Middle child — Fiction. 2. Families — Fiction. 3. Self-esteem — Fiction.]
I. Capps, Leigh, ill.   II. Title

To Krystal

Lydia sat on the steps of her house with her chin cupped in her hands and her bottom lip poked out as far as it could go. She tapped each finger against her cheek as she sulked and rolled her eyes at no one in particular.

"It's just not fair," she said aloud through clenched teeth. "My big sister is allowed to stay up late and go out with her friends. She chooses her own clothes and even baby-sits to make extra money."

"Kyle always gets a lot of attention because he's the baby," Lydia whined. "Whenever he does something new, everybody makes a big fuss over him."

"He doesn't have to make his bed, do homework, or practice music lessons. All he ever does is play and have fun."

"Here I am, stuck in the middle. Not the oldest, not the youngest - just stuck in the middle. Talk about *boring*."

9

Lydia picked up a broken branch and twirled it between her fingers. She sighed as she looked up and down the street but saw no one. There was no sign of life anywhere. The gentle breeze helped Lydia to take a deep breath.

"Where is everybody today?" she thought, and then remembered. "Kalid went to visit his grandparents and Sophie had a dentist appointment. I guess I'll just go for a walk."

Lydia stood and headed toward the end of her block, going nowhere in particular. With her hands plunged deep in her pockets and her head down, she kicked some leaves, twigs, a couple of rocks, and a soda can while paying absolutely no attention to where she was going.

Lydia continued up one street and down another. She said "Hello" to Mr. Gonzalez who was tending to his neatly manicured lawn. She waved to Mrs. Nelson who waved back through the shiny window she was cleaning.

"Ahhhh…" Lydia sighed. "There must be someone who will play with me today."

ydia decided to take a different route. She
imbed a few fences and carefully tip-toed
rough flower beds and herb gardens. But
e beautiful daffodils, daisies, and sunflowers
ere just too irresistable. "These will look
st lovely in my bedroom," she thought and
icked some of the perfect blossoms.

Lydia Johnson, you get out of the middle of
y garden, right *now!*" Lydia turned to see
Mrs. Meyers holding little Mitchell in one
rm and furiously shaking a tiny spoon in
er direction.

"Sorry, they are just so pretty," she mumbled
while walking away, deliberately trying to
avoid any more trouble.

"Ooooooops, Whoaaaa, Help! Hellllp! Get me out of here! Somebody help me!" Lydia shouted but her voice was muffled coming through a bundle of sheets, towels, pillowcases, bloomers and satin nightgowns. She punched and kicked and screamed until finally...

"Child, what are you doing? Are you all right?"
Mrs. Zimmerman came running to find Lydia buried in the middle of the clothes she had just laundered that morning. Lydia had walked right into the clothesline and was tangled up in one big mess. Mrs. Z (as the children liked to call her) pulled Lydia out of the heap and tried to fix her messy hair and rumpled clothes.

"I'm so sorry," Lydia gasped, trying to catch her breath.
"I wasn't watching where I was going."

"Well, be careful and pay attention, child. Now scoot. Go to the park and play and don't get into anymore trouble. Go on!" Mrs. Zimmerman shooed Lydia away then placed her hands on her hips and shook her head from side to side. "Tsk, Tsk, Tsk," was all she could say.

15

More dismal than ever, Lydia thought she should go to the park. Maybe there would be someone to play with and she could stay out of trouble. She was now well past her neighborhood and began to enjoy the wonderful sights, sounds, and smells of downtown. The aroma coming from Barbara's Bakery was delicious. Lydia closed her eyes, breathed in deeply and took a big whiff. "Ummmm. I'll get a jelly donut on my way back."

16

oot, tooooot, honk, honk… "Hey kid, get out of the way," someone yelled. Watch where you're going!"

ydia had wandered for several blocks when the voice startled her. She looked up only to nd herself in the middle of traffic on Main Street. "Oh my, I wasn't paying attention," ne mumbled, hurrying across the busy street. "Whew, close call."

ydia strolled past the bank, the deli, the print shop, the second-hand bookstore, the hinese restaurant, and Kelly's Dress Shop. She continued to browse and stroll…

Wham!!! Lydia didn't know what hit her when she tripped, tumbled, and landed in a big heap on the sidewalk.

"Are you all right?"

Lydia looked up to see several people standing over her. There were men in business suits and ties and ladies in skirts and high heel shoes.

"You bumped into a garbage can," someone said.

"You are in the middle of one big mess, little lady," came another voice.

"She seems to be a little dazed," Lydia heard one of the ladies say.

There she sat. In the middle of a pile of garbage. Yuck!

"I'm fine," Lydia said. She stood, brushed herself off as much as she could, made an attempt to fix her hair, and continued her journey.

Lydia headed home, more sullen than ever. Head down, shoulders drooped and a little bent over at the waist, she was indeed a sight. She forgot about the park and the jelly donut. She just wanted to go home.

Lydia sat on the steps, found the same twig she had been twirling earlier and felt even more sorry for herself.

Her heart leapt when she spotted her Dad coming home from work. *"Yes!"* she said to herself.

As he came closer, he took one look at Lydia and asked, "What's the matter, Pumpkin?"

"Nothing," she answered, slapping the broken branch against the step with a steady, slow, "whack… whack…"

Dad put down his briefcase, sat down beside Lydia and lifted her chin. "Come on. Tell me what's wrong."

"I hate being in the middle," she blurted out. "Kyle gets all the attention because he's the baby and Sissy gets to do whatever she wants because she's the oldest. The middle is NOT a good place to be. Believe me, *I know*," Lydia wailed as she remembered the adventures of her day.

21

Dad slowly leaned back against the step, crossed his legs and took a long, deep breath.

Lydia peeked at him out of the corner of her eye but continued to whack the broken branch against the step.

A few moments went by and then as if stricken by a great idea, Dad said, "Lydia, what's the best part of a sandwich?"

"Um, uh, I don't... the stuff in the middle," Lydia answered, somewhat startled.

"Dad always plays these games with me," she thought. "He gives me riddles and math problems just to see how quick I am. He's trying to change the subject. Didn't he hear anything I just said?"

Raising just one eyebrow, he questioned Lydia again. "What's the best part of a cookie?"

"The chocolate chips. Oh no, I mean the cream in the middle. That's my favorite."

Reaching over to gently lift the branch from Lydia's hand, Dad asked again, "What is your favorite fruit?"

"Bananas." Lydia wrinkled her forehead and looked at Dad with curious eyes.

"And, the best part of a banana is where?"

"In the middle," she answered. "But Dad..."

"Wait, wait, wait." Dad lifted his hand to quiet her.

"Do you like to read?" He persisted with the questions.

"Yes, you know how much I love books. That's a silly question."

Slowly, Lydia began to see her Dad's point, and although she wouldn't let him see, the corners of her mouth began to curl upward.

"Well then, tell me what the best part of any book is," Dad teased as he studied his fingernails.

Lydia had to think about this question. She was not sure if Dad was trying to trick her or not, but then she got it. "The pages in the middle!" she shouted, jumping up and getting excited.

Dad was getting excited about this too. "Now, when you receive a gift, although it's nicely wrapped in pretty paper and colorful bows, what's the best part?"

"The present in the middle!" Lydia screamed with delight.

"And... the best part of a frame?"

"A frame!!!!????"

"Yes."

"A frame... Let me think... Give me a hint, Dad, give me a hint."

"Think. You can do it."

Lydia's eyes widened and her jaw dropped. "The picture in the middle," she shouted.

27

"Dad, you know what?" she gasped, out of breath with delight.

"What?" he responded, pretending to be as thrilled as she was.

"We've been learning about oysters in science class and do you know what the best part of an oyster is?"

Dad slowly rubbed his chin... pondering, thinking... "I know!" he finally exclaimed. "The pearl in the middle!"

"You've got it!" Lydia plopped down and came to a conclusion. "You know, being in the middle is not so bad after all."

"I think you're right, Pumpkin... I think you're right," Dad said. "But wait. I have one more question. What's the best part of a donut?"

Lydia wrinkled her nose and gave her Dad a very puzzled look. "The hole in the middle?"

"No, the jelly," he said. "Let's go get one."

29

Lydia's heart danced as she walked down the street with her Dad. She noticed that her fingers felt so good, all covered up, right smack in the middle of his big strong hand.

"Lydia?"

"Yes?"

"What's that smell?"